This Walker book belongs to:

....

....

Many thanks to Amy, Chris, Kaylan and Caroline

First published in Great Britain 2010 by Walker Books Ltd
87 Vauxhall Walk, London SE11 5HJ

2 4 6 8 10 9 7 5 3 1

This book has been typeset in Malonia Voigo

Printed in Singapore

British Library Cataloguing in Publication Data:
a catalogue record for this book is available from the British Library

ISBN 978-1-4063-2491-4

www.walker.co.uk

GATOR

Randy Cecil

WALKER BOOKS
AND SUBSIDIARIES
LONDON • BOSTON • SYDNEY • AUCKLAND

Gator was once the happiest merry-go-round animal
in the world. He loved the flashing lights, the sound of the
fairground organ, and the feeling of the wind on his face.
But most of all, he loved the laughter.

In those days, the line for the merry-go-round seemed to go on for ever. All the children wanted to ride on Gator, Duck or the Golden Fish.

But times had changed.
Every day the crowd was smaller
than the day before.

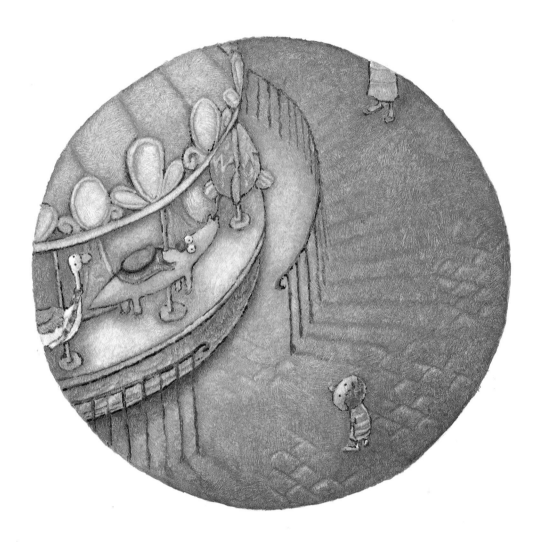

Finally, the fairground was all but forgotten.
The rides stopped running, the lights went dark,
and the laughter was gone. With nothing else to do,
Gator fell into a deep sleep.

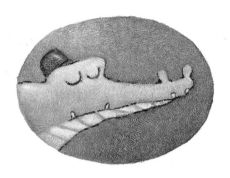

He slept and he slept.

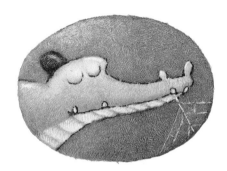

And as he slept, he dreamed that he was
once again whirling on the merry-go-round.
He could even feel the wind on his face.

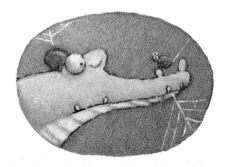

But it was only a spider attaching its web
to his snout. The merry-go-round was still quiet.
The fairground was still empty.

Unable to sleep any longer, Gator left his place on the merry-go-round. He touched the hole in his heart where the pole had been and looked out over the empty fairground. It was time to leave.

"But where will you go?" asked Duck.
"I'm not sure," Gator said.

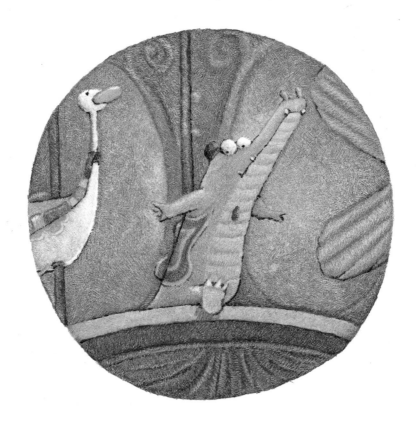

When he reached the fairground gate, he turned around and looked back at the merry-go-round, where he had spent his entire life. He looked at Duck, his friend, who had always been there, right behind him.

Then Gator opened the gate and
walked out into the world.

He was soon lost in a deep, dark forest.
He walked and walked until he knew every turn in
every path, every twist in every tree. A cold wind
blew through the hole in Gator's heart.

At last he came to a bridge. Some ducks
were swimming in the stream below.
"Well, look at that!" Gator said. "They look
just like my friend, Duck."

He leaned over to say hello with his biggest,
friendliest, toothiest smile.

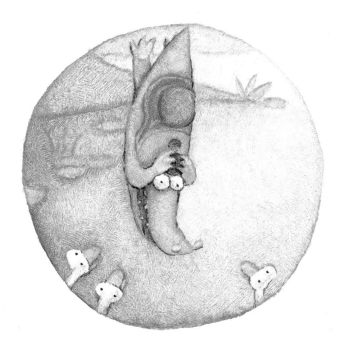

But he slipped, so instead of saying hello,
he said something more like "AAAGHEEEE!"

And the ducks flew away.

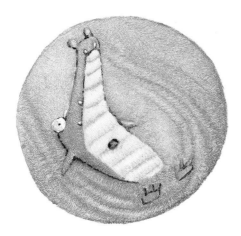

Gator hadn't known
that ducks could fly.
"How amazing!

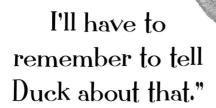

I'll have to
remember to tell
Duck about that."

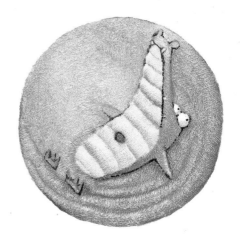

And then Gator heard something.

Laughter! It was coming from beyond a large open gate. "Maybe this is some sort of fairground!" Gator said as he walked inside.

But where were the flashing lights?

Where was the fairground organ?

Just as Gator began to think that it
was not a fairground after all,
he saw something amazing.
"Alligators!" he gasped.
"Maybe I should go in and say hello."

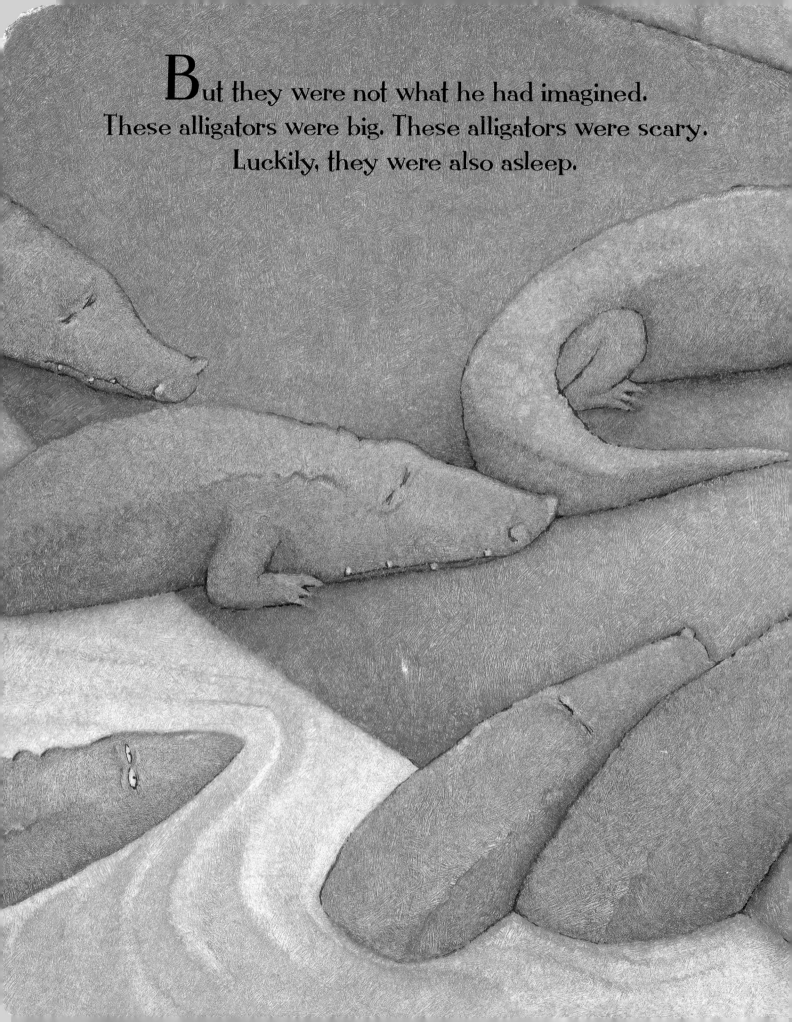

But they were not what he had imagined.
These alligators were big. These alligators were scary.
Luckily, they were also asleep.

Quickly, Gator tiptoed back out of the alligator pen.

Tears filled his eyes. He was tired
and lonely, and his search had led him nowhere.
He sat down on a bench and began to cry. He had
had enough. He wanted to go home.

Then Gator heard a little boy laughing.
"Daddy, what's that funny alligator doing
out here?" asked the boy.
"Why, that's no alligator," said the boy's father.
"That's Gator! He was my favourite animal
on the merry-go-round at the old fairground."
"Can we go there?" the little boy asked.
"I want to ride on Gator."

Gator jumped up. The fairground hadn't been forgotten! He could bring the laughter back. He began to lead the way to the merry-go-round. He was going home! More and more people followed.

On and on they went, back over the bridge and through the forest.

"Hello, Duck!" called Gator as he led
the people through the gates.

The fairground organ began to play, and the lights
came back on.

Gator took his place on the merry-go-round, with the little boy on his back. The hole in Gator's heart was gone.

He turned to tell Duck about his many adventures.
Did she know that ducks could fly?

As the merry-go-round whirled around,
laughter filled the fairground.
Everything was just the way
it used to be...

Except for Duck!